I LOVE YOU TO PIECES

By Nicole Johnson • Illustrated by Jason May

Random House New York

LEGO, the LEGO logo, the Brick and Knob configurations and the Minifigure
are trademarks and/or copyrights of the LEGO Group.
©2021 The LEGO Group. All rights reserved.
Manufactured under license granted to AMEET Sp. z o.o. by the LEGO Group.

AMEET Sp. z o.o.
Nowe Sady 6, 94–102 Łódź—Poland
ameet@ameet.eu
www.ameet.eu

www.LEGO.com

Published in the United States by Random House Children's Books, a division of Penguin Random House LLC, 1745 Broadway,
New York, NY 10019, and in Canada by Penguin Random House Canada Limited, Toronto. Random House and the colophon
are registered trademarks of Penguin Random House LLC.
rhcbooks.com
ISBN 978-0-593-43024-8 (trade) — ISBN 978-0-593-48106-6 (ebook)
Printed in the United States of America
10 9 8 7 6 5 4 3 2 1

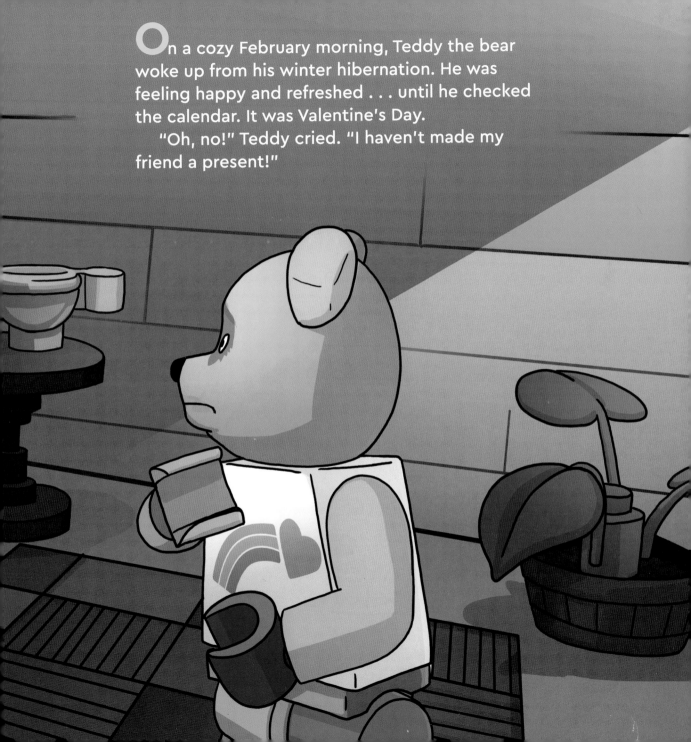

On a cozy February morning, Teddy the bear woke up from his winter hibernation. He was feeling happy and refreshed . . . until he checked the calendar. It was Valentine's Day.

"Oh, no!" Teddy cried. "I haven't made my friend a present!"

Teddy had made big plans for this Valentine's Day.
He was going to use this special day to show his friend
how much he loved him! But he had slept later than he
meant to and had no clue what to build for his friend.
He wondered what kind of present says "I love you."

Then Teddy got an idea. He would go out and ask other people about the gifts they made for Valentine's Day! Surely someone else had given the perfect gift.

Teddy's friend loved to swim, so Teddy headed to the sea in a rowboat to look for inspiration. He found a pair of merpeople there and asked them what they'd given each other for Valentine's Day.

"I gave him a bracelet made of seashells,"
one merperson said.

"And I gathered some seaweed for us to
snack on together," said the other.

Teddy thought about when he and his friend spent time together. His friend always wanted to play games. While the bracelet and seaweed snacks were perfect gifts for the merpeople, they weren't quite right for his friend.

"Thanks for your help,"
Teddy said. "But I think I need
to keep looking."
With a wave goodbye,
Teddy rowed back to shore.

Next, Teddy headed to a nearby old western town. He met a pair of cowboys, who greeted him with a friendly "Howdy!"
"What do you two like to get for Valentine's Day?" Teddy asked.

"For any holiday, all I need is a new hat," one said.
"Or maybe a pair of shiny boots," said the other.

Teddy knew that boots were not the right gift for his friend.
They look great on a cowboy, but bears don't wear shoes!

Next, Teddy thought about the hat. His friend loved getting dressed up!

But when Teddy tried on the cowboy's hat, it didn't fit over his ears! He returned the hat to the cowboy.

Teddy had one more idea. Scientists are great at finding answers to hard questions! Maybe a scientist could help. So Teddy went to a scientist's lab and asked what he should do.

"I've just invented a robot that I think can help," the scientist said.

She led Teddy to a shiny new robot and turned it on.
"This robot can answer any question!" she exclaimed.

"How do I find the perfect Valentine's Day gift for my
friend?" Teddy asked hopefully.

The robot sprang to life with blinking lights and whirring noises. "The asker must study the subject thoroughly to make a proper gift hypothesis," said the robot. Then it shut down.

"There you have it!" the scientist said, satisfied and already moving on to her next experiment.

But Teddy had no idea what that meant! Stumped, he left the lab.

Teddy spent the whole day talking to different people.

Their ideas sounded interesting and fun, but none of them were quite right for his friend.

Back at home, Teddy thought about his day. Everyone had talked about the perfect gift for *them*, but what's perfect for a merperson or a cowboy would never be the right gift for his friend.

Then Teddy understood. Nothing was right because every gift is special for the person receiving it. He needed to think about his friend—just like the robot had tried to tell him!

Teddy thought about his friend and what he loved. He loved playing games, dressing up in fun costumes, and eating berries.

"Aha!" Teddy exclaimed. He was going to make his friend their own special game!

Teddy had no time to waste. He gathered everything he needed and got to work building the best present ever!

Ta-da! Teddy had built a costume trunk and filled it with silly clothes. For his game, each bear would create their own costume. Whoever made the funniest costume would win a berry!

Proud of his gift, Teddy carried it to his friend's house. But
it was very heavy, and just as Teddy knocked on the door . . .

. . . he dropped the present!

Teddy's friend opened the door at that moment. Teddy was heartbroken.

"Oh, Teddy," said his friend. "This was so thoughtful, but I don't need a gift. I love you anyway! In fact, I love you to *pieces*. And now we have an even better gift— we get to build something new together!"

Sharing a smile, the friends got to work building an all-new game. It wasn't the Valentine's Day Teddy had planned for, but it was just as perfect as he had imagined it would be.